A

ANTICS!

Z

ANTICS!

An Alphabetical **Anthology**

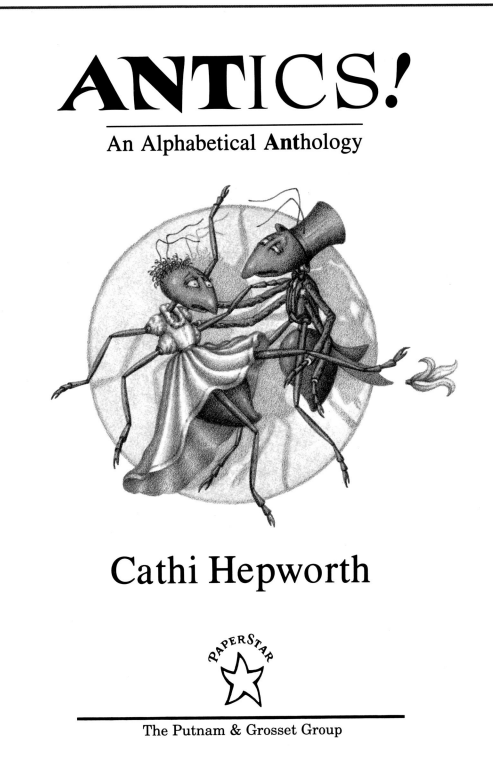

Cathi Hepworth

PAPERSTAR

The Putnam & Grosset Group

A

A PaperStar Book, published in 1996 by The Putnam & Grosset Group,
200 Madison Avenue, New York, NY 10016.
PaperStar and the PaperStar logo are trademarks of The Putnam Berkley Group, Inc.
Originally published in 1992 by G. P. Putnam's Sons, New York.
Published simultaneously in Canada. Printed in the United States of America.
Library of Congress Cataloging-in-Publication Data
Hepworth, Catherine.
Antics!: an alphabet of ants/by Cathi Hepworth. p.   cm.
Summary: Alphabetical entries from A to Z all have an "ant" somewhere
in the word: There's E for Enchanter, P for Pantaloons, S for Santa
Claus, and Y for Your Ant Yetta.
1. English language—Alphabet—Juvenile literature.
[1. Alphabet.]   I. Title.   PE1155.H47   1992   91-2672   CIP AC
421.1—dc 20
ISBN 0-698-11350-0
1   3   5   7   9   10   8   6   4   2

Printed on recycled paper

Z

For Brad,
and for Mom, Dad, Dave,
John, Jenni, Becki, and Ami…
"the Neandersons"

Antique

Brilliant

Chant

Deviant

Enchanter

F l a m b o y **a n t**

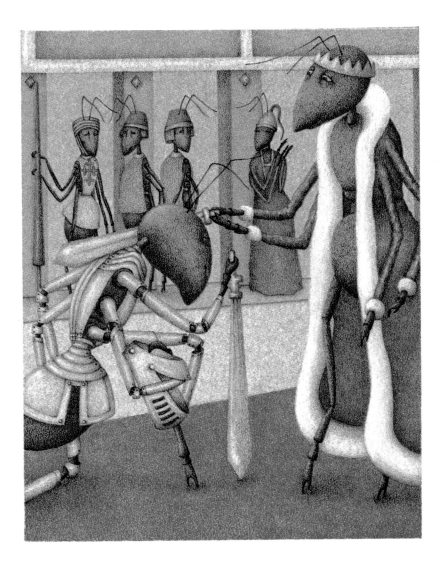

Gallant

Hesitant

Immigrants

Jubil**ant**

Kant

L ieuten ant

Mutant

Nonchalant

Observ**ant**

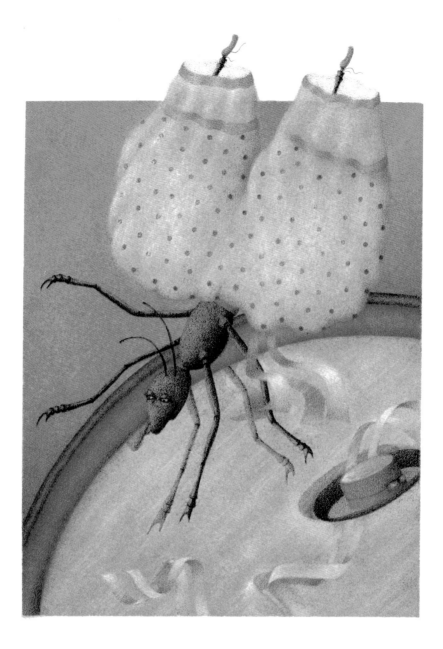

Pantaloons

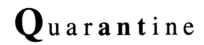

Quarantine

Rembrant

S a n t a C l a u s

Tan**t**r**u**m

Unpleas**ant**

Vigil**a**nt**es**

Wanted

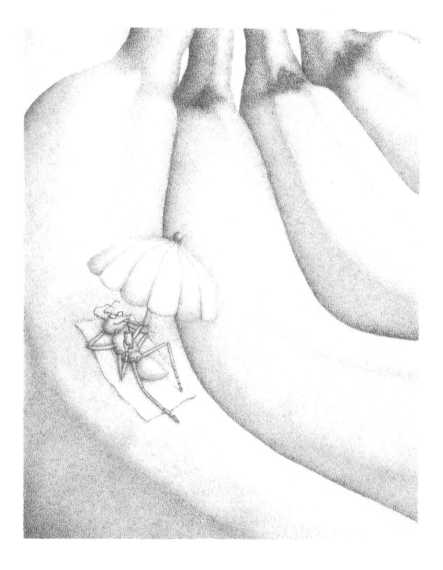

Xanthophile

Your **A**nt Yetta

Antzzzzzz**Z**